To Teddy—tiny dog with a big heart

GROSSET & DUNLAP
Published by the Penguin Group
Penguin Group (USA) Inc., 375 Hudson Street, New York, New York 10014, USA

USA | Canada | UK | Ireland | Australia | New Zealand | India | South Africa | China
Penguin Books Ltd, Registered Offices: 80 Strand, London WC2R 0RL, England

For more information about the Penguin Group visit penguin.com

Text copyright © 2008 Sue Bentley. Illustrations copyright © 2008 Angela Swan.
Cover illustration copyright © 2008 Andrew Farley. First printed in Great Britain in 2008
by Penguin Books Ltd. First published in the United States in 2013 by Grosset & Dunlap, a
division of Penguin Young Readers Group, 345 Hudson Street, New York, New York 10014.
GROSSET & DUNLAP is a trademark of Penguin Group (USA) Inc. Printed in the U.S.A.

Library of Congress Cataloging-in-Publication Data is available.

ISBN 978-0-448-46737-5   10 9 8 7 6 5 4 3 2

Snowy Wishes

SUE BENTLEY

Illustrated by Angela Swan

Grosset & Dunlap
An Imprint of Penguin Group (USA) Inc.

Prologue

Storm rolled on his back on the
stony ground. The young silver-gray wolf
enjoyed the scratchy feeling against his
thick fur. It felt good to be back in his
homeland.

Suddenly, a fierce howl rose into the
air and echoed over the quiet hillside.

"Shadow!" gasped Storm. The fierce
lone wolf who had attacked Storm's

Moon-claw pack was very close. He
should have known that it wasn't safe
to return.

There was a flash of bright gold
light and a silent explosion of gold
sparks. The young wolf disappeared
and in its place stood a tiny, fluffy
white Labrador puppy with floppy
ears and big midnight-blue eyes.

Storm's short puppy legs trembled.
He needed to find somewhere to hide,
and quickly.

Halfway up the slope, thick bushes
clung to the rough ground. Storm
raced toward them, his little paws
kicking up spurts of dust. A dark wolf
shape was crouching near one of the
bushes. Storm's breath caught in his
throat with terror, and he skidded

sideways in an attempt to escape.

"In here, my son," the wolf called in a deep, gentle growl.

"Mother!" Storm yapped with relief.

He stopped and raced back toward the bush where she was hiding. As he reached her, Storm's whole body wriggled and his silky little tail wagged delightedly.

Canista reached out a huge paw and gathered her disguised pup close against her warm body. She licked Storm's fluffy white muzzle. "I am glad to see you again, but you cannot stay. Shadow is looking for you. He wants to lead the Moon-claw pack, but the others will not follow him while you live."

Storm's midnight-blue eyes sparked

with anger and fear. "He has already killed my father and brothers and wounded you. I will fight Shadow and make him leave our lands."

Canista showed her strong, sharp teeth in a proud smile. "Bravely said, but Shadow is too strong for you, and I am still weak from his poisoned bite and cannot help you. Go back to the other world. Hide there and return when you are wiser and your magic is stronger."

Storm whined softly. He knew his mother was right, but he hated to leave her.

He huffed out a warm puppy breath that glittered with a thousand tiny gold sparks. The healing mist swirled round Canista's paw and then sank into her thick gray fur.

"Thank you, Storm. The pain is much better," she rumbled softly.

Suddenly, another terrifying howl rang out and there came the sound of enormous paws thudding up the slope toward them.

"I know you are there, Storm. Let us finish this!" growled a harsh, cruel voice.

"Go now! Save yourself!" Canista urged.

Storm whimpered as he felt the power gathering inside his tiny form. Bright gold sparks ignited in his fluffy white fur. A bright gold light spread around him. And grew brighter . . .

Chapter
ONE

"Robyn, sweetheart. Are you awake?"

At the sound of her mom's voice in the doorway, Robyn Parsons sat up slowly. Her bunk was moving very slightly with the motion of the ship. From somewhere deep below her, she could hear the faint rumbling of the *Sea Princess*'s enormous engines.

"I wasn't asleep. I was just resting,"

Robyn murmured. "Uh-oh," she breathed as her tummy gave a familiar lurch.

"Still feeling weak and wobbly?" Mrs. Parsons said gently. "Poor old you. That's nearly two days you've been stuck in here."

"I know," Robyn said glumly, feeling very down in the dumps.

She'd been looking forward to this Christmas even more than usual.

Robyn didn't have any brothers or

sisters, and her dad worked away from home a lot. This was the first chance in ages to spend lots of time with him, and they would all be together as a family.

"I think we deserve a vacation with guaranteed snow, lights, and lots of atmosphere! Leave it to me," Mr. Parsons had declared.

And now here they all were, all aboard the *Sea Princess* for a winter cruise around the wild and beautiful coast of Norway.

Robyn sighed. At this rate, she was going to be lucky if she caught a glimpse of any snowcapped mountains through the cabin window, let alone spend any time with her dad. It looked like this was going to be another lonely Christmas after all.

"How come you and Dad are okay? I can barely even stand up without wanting to throw up," she grumbled.

"It's just sheer bad luck," her mom said sympathetically. "We had no idea

that you'd react so badly to a sea voyage, or we'd have chosen a different way of spending Christmas." She handed Robyn a glass. "Have a drink of water. It might help."

Robyn sipped the water. She felt a tiny bit better after having a drink. "Thanks, Mom. I think I might stay sitting up. Maybe I'll look through that music magazine you got me. Where's Dad?"

"In the sun lounge, reading his paper. Are you sure you wouldn't like me to bring you something? Maybe a sandwich or some fruit?"

At the thought of food, Robyn made a face. "I couldn't eat a thing."

Mrs. Parsons shook her head slowly. "I'm really starting to wonder whether

we shouldn't get off the ship at the
next port and arrange to take you home."

"No! You can't!" Robyn said at once
and then wished that she hadn't spoken
so loudly. Her head felt as if it was
spinning. "Dad will be so disappointed
if we waste this vacation. And you've
been really looking forward to it for
ages."

"So have you, sweetheart," her mom
reminded her gently. "This was supposed
to be a really special Christmas together,
remember?"

Robyn nodded. "I know, but we'll
have lots more of them," she said, trying
hard to hide her disappointment for her
mom's sake. "I don't see why you and
Dad can't still have a good time. I'll be
fine in here by myself. I'm nearly ten

years old, aren't I? And I *have* to start feeling better soon. No one stays seasick forever!"

Mrs. Parsons shook her head slowly. "I'm still not happy about leaving you alone. I'm just going to pop back to have a word with your dad. Let's see what he has to say about this. I won't be long."

Robyn's shoulders slumped as the cabin door closed. Even though it wasn't her fault that she felt so ill, she knew she'd feel really guilty if their cruise was cut short.

It's just not fair! I'm so fed up of being sick! she grumbled to herself.

She took a deep breath and decided to get up. Maybe her mom and dad would change their minds about taking her home if she could convince them that she was feeling stronger.

Pushing back her quilt, Robyn slowly swung her legs over the side of her bunk. Her head swam a bit, but she stood up determinedly and reached for her jeans and fleece top. She was a bit wobbly on her feet, but she took her time getting dressed and finally managed it okay.

I'm much better. I'm fine, she told herself determinedly as she bent down to pull on her sneakers. Suddenly, a strong dizzy feeling washed over her, and she lost her balance.

"Oh," Robyn gasped, toppling forward.

She threw out her arms, ready for a painful bruising landing, when a brilliant golden flash and a shower of sparks lit up the small cabin. Time

seemed to stand still and a warm tingling
sensation ran down Robyn's spine. She
felt a sudden jolt, but there was no hard
landing.

To her complete astonishment,
Robyn found herself sprawled full-length
on her tummy on a sort of bouncy
raft, made of shimmering gold-colored
bubbles, and whizzing all around her was

an ice storm of spinning, glittering sparks.

Robyn caught her breath as she felt herself slowly rising up into a sitting position and then being lowered gently on to the floor. The bubble raft and sparks dissolved with a loud crackling noise, like chip bags being crumpled up.

Robyn sat there shakily on the floor and looked around nervously.

What had just happened? She felt like pinching herself to see if she had been dreaming.

"I hope you are not hurt," woofed a strange little voice.

Robyn nearly jumped out of her skin. "Who said that?" She twisted around, her eyes searching the small cabin.

Crouching on top of the neat chest of drawers opposite, Robyn saw a tiny, fluffy white puppy, with cute floppy ears, a silky white tail, and midnight-blue eyes. Thousands of tiny diamond-bright golden sparkles glittered in its thick fur.

C h a p t e r
TWO

Robyn's eyes widened. Her mom must have brought in the cute toy to cheer her up and then forgotten to tell her about it. She must be more affected by her seasickness than she'd realized—first she'd imagined floating on a sparkly bubble raft, and now she thought she'd heard this toy puppy speak to her!

Robyn stood up and went to reach

out toward the toy. "Hello. Aren't you gorgeous? I wonder where Mom found you."

"I came here by myself," the puppy woofed. "When you fell, I used my magic to stop you from being hurt. I am sorry if I startled you."

Robyn gasped and pulled her hand back as if it had been burned. "You . . . you *can* talk!" she cried.

The puppy blinked up at her with wide midnight-blue eyes. Despite its tiny size, it didn't seem to be afraid of her.

"Yes. I am Storm of the Moon-claw pack. What is your name? And what is this strange moving place?"

"Robyn. Robyn Parsons. And we're on a ship called *Sea Princess*. I'm here on a Christmas cruise with my parents," Robyn explained, her mind still whirling. She found it difficult to take all this in, but she didn't want to scare the amazing puppy away. "Um . . . I don't know what you did just now, but thanks for helping me. I could have hurt myself badly."

"You are welcome," Storm yapped.

Robyn slowly backed up to the edge of her bunk and then sat down. "Sorry, I'm feeling a bit sick. I've been like this since we came on board."

Storm's little pointed face clouded with concern. "I will make you better."

Robyn instantly felt another warm tingling sensation down her back as Storm reached out one fluffy, little white paw and sent a fountain of tiny sparks toward her. They whirled around her, humming like tiny worker bees before disappearing. She felt the sickness washing downward and draining out of her toes, just as if she'd been standing under the flow of a warm shower.

"Wow! That's amazing," she cried delightedly, jumping up. "I don't feel sick anymore, and I'm not dizzy or anything! Thanks again, Storm!"

"That is good." Storm grinned, showing his sharp little teeth, and then his face took on a serious expression. "I need to hide now, Robyn. Can you help me?"

"I'd love to, but why do you need to do that?" Robyn asked, looking down at the cute white puppy, who was beginning to tremble all over.

Storm's midnight-blue eyes darkened with anger. "An evil lone wolf attacked our Moon-claw pack—he is called Shadow. Shadow killed my father and brothers and wounded my mother. He wants to lead our pack, but the others are waiting for me."

"But how can you lead a wolf pack? You're a tiny pu—" Robyn began.

"Stand back, please!" Storm interrupted.

There was a dazzling flare of golden light, which blinded Robyn for a moment. For a second or two, she couldn't see anything. But when her

sight cleared, the cute white puppy had
gone and in its place a magnificent young
silver-gray wolf stood proudly, almost
filling the whole of the tiny cabin. Its
thick neck-ruff glittered all over as if it
had been dipped in gold dust.

Robyn caught her breath and would
have backed away if there had been
room. "Storm?" she gasped, eyeing the

young wolf's sharp teeth, strong muscles, and huge powerful paws.

"Yes, it is me. Do not be afraid. I will not harm you," Storm replied in a deep, velvety growl.

Robyn had hardly got used to the great majestic wolf when there was a final flash of dazzling light. A shower of bright sparks crackled harmlessly down around her and Storm reappeared as a cute, fluffy white puppy.

"Wow! You really are a wolf! That's an amazing disguise," Robyn whispered.

Storm tucked his little white tail between his legs, and Robyn saw that he was beginning to tremble again. "Shadow will recognize me if he finds out I'm here, and then he will use his magic against me. Please will you help?"

Robyn's soft heart went out to the tiny scared puppy. She bent down and stroked his soft little head. Storm was impressive as his real self, but in his cute puppy disguise he was totally adorable.

"Of course I'll help you and—" Robyn stopped as she realized something. "Oh, I don't think animals are allowed on board. I could try to hide you in my cabin, but it's small and you'll be really bored if you have to stay in there for the whole time."

"I can come everywhere with you. I will use my magic so that only you can see and hear me," Storm woofed eagerly. A couple of tiny sparks danced around his floppy white ears and then blinked out. "It is done."

"You've made yourself invisible?

Cool!" Robyn said delightedly. She picked
Storm up and gave him a cuddle. His
white fur was thick and silky and smelled
of cold fresh air. "Let's go and explore *Sea
Princess* together!"

"I would like that!" Storm's little white muzzle wrinkled in a smile, and he licked her chin with his pink tongue.

"I can't wait to go and find Mom and Dad and tell them about you." Robyn smiled down at him.

"No!" Storm's face was suddenly serious. "You can never tell anyone my secret. Promise me," he woofed gently.

Robyn felt disappointed that she couldn't share the news about her wonderful new friend with her parents— she was sure they would love him, too. But if it would help to keep the tiny puppy safe, Robyn decided to keep this secret to herself.

"Okay. I won't say anything. Cross my heart."

"What's this promise you're making?"

said Mr. Parsons, coming into the cabin.

"Dad!" Robyn whirled around in
shock to see her mom and dad standing
there. She'd been so busy talking to
Storm that she hadn't heard the cabin
door open. "I was just promising . . .
um . . . myself," she said, thinking
quickly. "That I was . . . um . . . going
to have the best time ever, now that I

feel better. Because I've got lots of time to make up, haven't I?"

"You certainly have," her dad said, looking surprised but delighted. "Well, I must say that you seem to have made a miracle recovery. And there your mom was, wondering whether we ought to take you home!"

Robyn still couldn't quite believe that her mom and dad hadn't noticed Storm in her arms. But when neither of them said anything about the tiny puppy, she felt herself starting to relax.

"No one's going home. So there!" Robyn exclaimed, her eyes shining.

She spun around and pretended to straighten her quilt, giving Storm the chance to jump onto her bunk.

When Robyn turned back to her

parents, her mom was beaming at her. "I can hardly believe it. You're like a totally different girl than the one I was talking to just a few minutes ago. It's just like magic!"

If only Mom knew how right she was, Robyn thought, smiling inwardly.

"Well, you look ready to leave the cabin at last. I expect you'd like a look around to see what you've been missing. Where do you feel like going?" her dad asked.

Robyn's tummy rumbled, and she realized that she was starving.

"Lunch it is, then!" said her mom.

As Robyn followed her parents to an upper deck, Storm trotted invisibly at her heel. Robyn had a warm glow inside. After a false start, her vacation

was just beginning, and she now had a
wonderful new friend to share it with, too.

Chapter
THREE

"Doesn't everywhere look great?"
Robyn said to Storm. "It makes me feel all
Christmassy."

They were walking across a part of the
ship with a domed ceiling and
large picture windows, swathed with
evergreen garlands. Lanterns and
traditional decorations made of wood
and tin were strung around the walls

and Christmas trees gleamed with
hundreds of twinkly lights.

Robyn peered through one of the
large windows. The Norwegian sky was
filled with a strange dark-gray light and
the heavy, rolling sea looked like a sheet of
ridged silver.

"It's really weird to think that it never
gets completely light during the day in
winter. I don't know if I'd like to live here
all year round," she whispered to Storm.
"But it looks amazing, doesn't it? Like
something out of a fairy tale. You can just
imagine scaly monsters in the sea and

fierce trolls and frost giants living in the mountains."

"Trolls and frost giants?" Storm flattened his ears and his silky white tail drooped.

Robyn grinned. "Sorry. I didn't mean to scare you. I read about Viking legends and stuff when I knew we were coming here on vacation."

Storm still seemed unsure about being aboard a ship. He reared up on to his back legs beside her and pressed his little nose to the window. His big midnight-blue eyes widened, and he gave a worried little whine.

"Are you okay?" Robyn asked, wishing she hadn't mentioned giants and trolls now. She hadn't realized that Storm would take her seriously.

"I think we are lost," Storm woofed. "There is so much gray water and sky, but I cannot see any land."

"That's because we're looking out on to open sea on this side," Robyn explained. "We can go up on deck, if you like, and then you'll be able to see land and mountains."

Storm nodded, still not looking entirely happy as he jumped back down.

Robyn didn't expect that any of the magical wolves from the Moon-claw pack had ever been on a cruise ship; or on any other kind of ship for that matter. In his home world, Storm never left land. No wonder he was ill at ease.

"Come on, let's catch up with Mom and Dad," she said to Storm, changing the subject. "I could eat a horse!"

Storm's face showed surprise. "A horse? I have seen one of those. It was very large!"

"I know. I wouldn't really want to eat one. It's just something that people say when they're really hungry!"

Storm's little white muzzle twitched
in a grin. Robyn was pleased to see
that his anxious look had completely
disappeared.

"I am very hungry, too!" he yapped,
falling into step with Robyn as she set off
again.

A buzz of conversation and a riot
of delicious smells greeted them as they
entered the restaurant. Robyn could see
her mom and dad beginning to help
themselves from the buffet area. She
picked up a tray and joined them.

"Wow! Look at all this!" she
whispered to Storm, her mouth watering.
"I hardly know what to choose."

There was an enormous display of
food with hot and cold dishes of all
kinds, salads, sandwiches, desserts, cakes,

and baskets of fruit and chocolates. In
the center there was an entire miniature
village made of iced gingerbread and
an amazing ice sculpture of a polar bear.

Robyn heaped her plate with food
for her and Storm, and then followed
her mom and dad to an empty table.
As soon as she sat down, Storm jumped
up on to her lap and curled up.

After almost two days of just drinking
water, Robyn ate hungrily. She slipped
bits of meat and fish under the table
to Storm without her mom and dad
noticing.

"Human food tastes very good,"
Storm woofed, licking his chops when
he'd finished. "Thank you, Robyn."

Robyn's mom and dad were
wondering what to do next. "We could

go swimming or watch a movie or even have a sauna," her mom said. "There's a game room, shops, an Internet café, and lots of organized events, too."

"Could we go up on deck and look at the view?" Robyn asked. If Storm could see that they weren't far from land, he might feel less nervous about being on *Sea Princess*.

"Fine by me," her mom said. "I think we should be steaming through a fjord by now. It should be quite spectacular."

Up on deck a cold wind was blowing, and Robyn wrapped her coat around Storm to keep him warm. The tiny puppy was peeping out from the front opening and Robyn could feel him snuggled against her chest, like a fluffy hot-water bottle.

Sea Princess was moving up a wide
channel that had been created thousands
of years ago by melting glaciers. The
fjord stretched deep into the surrounding
mountains. Painted wooden houses
were clustered on the slopes and the
towering, snowcapped tops were hidden
by clouds.

Some people sat on deck in chairs,
bundled up in warm blankets as they
enjoyed the dramatic scenery. Others
were lining the ship's rail, pointing
out details to each other and taking
photographs.

Robyn found a place to stand at the
rail and looked down at the gray-green
water, far below. "I wonder how deep it is
here," she commented to Storm.

"Some of these fjords are almost four

thousand feet deep," her dad said, coming to stand beside her. "That's as deep as the mountains you can see."

Robyn realized that she must have spoken more loudly than she'd intended to, and her dad had thought she was speaking to him. She would have to be more careful about keeping Storm's secret.

"That's scarily deep," she said to her dad.

Some way further on, the ship slowly rounded a bend and Robyn saw a waterfall gushing from a gorge in a high cliff. Jagged icicles, like spears, hung down from the rock and the foaming curtain of water fell straight down between them.

"Warm enough, honey?" her dad asked cheerfully. "This icy air's really bringing the color back to your cheeks."

"I feel fine. I don't mind the cold that much," Robyn said, giving her dad a hug. Storm gave a little warning squeak as he got a bit squashed between the two of them. "Sorry!" Robyn whispered to him, when her dad broke away.

"Well, I've had enough of it for now,"

her mom said with a shiver. "I think I might have a sauna to warm me up."

"That's a good idea. I'll come with you. What about you, Robyn?" her dad asked.

Robyn shook her head. "No, thanks." She didn't like all that hot steam, and she didn't want to leave Storm by himself. "I think I'll stay out here for a while. I'll come and meet you at the fitness center."

"All right, honey," her mom said. "By the way, the ship's docking at a fairly big town this afternoon. I thought we could all go ashore and do some shopping."

"Sounds great. Enjoy your sauna. See you later," Robyn called as her parents walked away. Now that she felt well enough to spend some time with her mom and dad, she definitely didn't mind wandering around by herself with Storm.

Her dad looked over his shoulder and winked at her. "Watch out for trolls."

Robyn grinned. "I will!"

She didn't notice Storm shrinking further down inside her coat, his dewy eyes looking around nervously.

The fjord began to get narrower and more winding. The sides of the mountains were steeper here, without any houses or farms. Ice and snow clung to the jagged black rock face and the gray clouds seemed lower.

Robyn was quite enjoying the gloomy landscape. It was easy to believe that fierce trolls lay in wait for unwary travelers.

Suddenly, a bloodcurdling cry rang out behind her. Robyn almost jumped out of her skin, and Storm yelped in terror. Robyn whipped around to see a number of hairy men with huge teeth, pointed ears, and lumpy faces running toward her across the deck. They were dressed in rough fur cloaks and shaking their fists.

"Trolls!" gasped Robyn.

Storm growled, his whole body tensing inside Robyn's coat.

Robyn's heart beat fast. Some of the other passengers screamed and one little girl hid behind her dad.

And then Robyn saw one of the "trolls" adjusting his mask and another one of them straightening his hairy wig. It was just some of the ship's crew who had dressed up to put on a special performance for the passengers.

She started to laugh. "It's okay, Storm. It's only . . . ," she began in a reassuring voice, but it was too late.

Robyn felt a familiar, warm prickling sensation down her spine as big gold sparks flowered in Storm's fluffy white fur and his ears crackled with magical power.

Something very strange was about to happen.

Chapter
FOUR

Robyn watched in complete amazement as Storm leaped out of her coat and sprang on to the deck, trailing a comet's tail of gold sparks.

He lifted one tiny front paw and sent a huge spray of glittering sparks whooshing into the icy air. Robyn saw them hang there for a second and then transform into grayish smoke, which sank down on to the trolls in the thickest mist she had ever seen.

"Hey! What's going on?" one of them cried from the middle of the dense mist.

"Oops, sorry," said another one, as he tripped over his friend.

They couldn't see where they were going. Robyn could hear the disguised crew members staggering around and bumping into each other. The other passengers thought it was all part of the

act and began laughing and cheering them on.

But as the magical mist spread, they became swallowed up in it, too.

"Follow me, Robyn! I will save you from the monsters," Storm yapped. His little form glowed as brightly as a lantern as he scampered toward the door to the lower deck.

"Come back, Storm!" Robyn called to him above all the noise. "They're not real trolls. They're people dressed up. It's just for fun!"

Storm stopped dead and then padded back toward her. In the little pool of light made by his magically glowing body, Robyn could see a shamefaced expression creep over his fluffy white face.

"I am sorry. I thought that you were in danger," Storm yapped quietly, flattening his ears.

"It's okay. I know you were only trying to protect me, but I think you'd better make the fog disappear now," she said gently.

Storm nodded.

He sent a big spurt of bright gold sparks whooshing across the deck. The sparkles were like a powerful jet spray at a car wash, magically blasting the fog into thin strands. Seconds later it all blew away on the icy wind.

The disguised crewmen stood there on the clear deck, looking puzzled. Their wigs were all crooked and their troll masks were dangling around their necks. But they soon recovered.

Straightening their costumes, they
skipped around the deck, roaring and
waving their arms.

Delighted applause broke out as
more of the crew came on to the deck,
holding trays of hot drinks, food, and
snacks.

"You must pay the price for entering
our land," one of the trolls boomed,
grinning broadly. "We order you to
feast with us on troll brew and hot troll
soup!"

As everyone began helping
themselves, Robyn decided that this was
a good time for her and Storm to make
their exit.

Later that afternoon after *Sea Princess*
docked at the harbor, Robyn, Storm

and her mom and dad went ashore. They
caught a bus to the south of the city with
lots of other people on the cruise.

Robyn sat with Storm safely inside
the shoulder bag on her lap. He stuck
his head out to look at the broad, snow-
covered streets and modern shops and
offices.

Robyn could see colored lights
gleaming from house windows, and
there were lots of green wreaths hung

on doors. Here and there, they passed traditional wooden buildings, painted in shades of red, orange, or mustard.

"Everything looks so Christmassy here. I love it," she whispered. "I hope I can get some presents for Mom and Dad."

Storm twisted round and looked up at her. "What is Christmas?"

"Oh, of course. I don't suppose you have it in your world, do you?" Robyn realized. "Christmas is a special time when we celebrate the baby Jesus being born. We sing carols, and families all get together and exchange presents and eat lots of yummy food. Dad usually stuffs himself with turkey, stuffing, and pie and then moans about his pants being tight! At least, that's what we usually do at home. It's going to seem a bit different this year. We celebrate Christmas on Christmas Eve aboard *Sea Princess.*"

Storm looked a bit puzzled, but his midnight-blue eyes were twinkling with excitement. "It sounds very odd, but I think I will enjoy Christmas, especially the food!"

The bus stopped near an enormous cathedral with a towering spire and lots of amazing stone carving. Colored light streamed out on to the snow from its stained-glass windows.

Robyn's mom produced a tourist brochure she'd picked up on the way to the bus. "I think I'd like to look around inside that cathedral. It says here that it's almost a thousand years old. Imagine that!" she said enthusiastically.

"Wow!" Robyn said. She couldn't
imagine anything being that old. But she
didn't really want to walk around some
musty-smelling old cathedral for hours,
however impressive it was. "Do we all have

to go?" she asked, without enthusiasm.

Mr. Parsons smiled. "I don't think so. I'm not as interested in old buildings as your mom. You and I'll go shopping and meet her later."

"Oh good," Robyn said, relieved.

"Fine," Mrs. Parsons said. "I'm quite happy to wander by myself." She turned to her husband. "I'll see you back here in a couple of hours?"

Mr. Parsons nodded. "Sounds good."

Robyn waved to her mum as she set off toward the cathedral, and then she and her dad set off in search of interesting shops. Storm leaned up and hooked his front paws over her shoulder bag, so that he could look at the surroundings.

They had been walking for a couple of minutes when Storm reached out and tapped Robyn's arm with one front paw. She looked down to see that he'd pricked up his little ears.

"I can hear music," he yapped.

"I can, too," Robyn whispered. "Can you hear that, Dad?" she said in a louder voice. "It's coming from over there."

Mr. Parsons listened. "Oh yes. It's quite faint, but it sounds like folk music. Let's go and have a look."

As they walked to the end of the street, the music got louder. They reached a cobbled square, surrounded by stalls heaped with crystallized fruit, gingerbread, and spiced cookies. Cheery lanterns were strung between the buildings encircling the small square, and green garlands and decorations were looped between the stalls.

Storm yipped excitedly as he saw the bandstand, with musicians playing violins. Women in colorful felt skirts and men in vests and buckled shoes were dancing. A festive smell of spiced wine and roasted nuts filled the frosty air.

"Oh, it's a Christmas festival!" Robyn exclaimed delightedly.

Chapter
FIVE

Robyn sipped a cup of hot spiced apple juice as she watched some children building snowmen. It was a competition, and a number of half-built snow trolls and elves stood in one corner of the square. There was even a Santa Claus snowman with his snow reindeer.

In the strange half-light, the glowing lanterns cast a cheerful glow over

everything. Storm jumped out of Robyn's
bag in another little flurry of sparks.

At first, Robyn was worried that his
little paws would get cold on the frozen
ground. But Storm's white ears sizzled
with tiny sparks, and she noticed that he
was now wearing four tiny furry boots.

He looked so cute wearing them
that Robyn burst out laughing, which
she quickly turned into a cough. She

didn't want to hurt her puppy friend's
feelings.

As she and her dad wandered around
the market stalls, they bought cheese,
chocolate, and spice cakes for presents to
take home for Gran and Gramps. Robyn
didn't see anything she wanted to buy
for her mom and dad.

She spotted a shop on the other side
of the square. "I'm just going to head
over to that shop over there. I won't be
long," she told her dad.

Mr. Parsons nodded. "All right. I'll
still be here."

Storm scampered after Robyn as she
headed across the square. Inside the shop,
it felt really warm after the cold outside.
Robyn took off her hat and gloves and
stuffed them in her coat pocket.

There were lots of people looking at
the gifts and cuddly toys. Robyn noticed
a rack of knitwear. Maybe her mom
would like a traditional hand-knitted
cardigan.

As she went to have a closer look,
Robyn heard raised voices. A sales
assistant was speaking sharply to a tall,
slim girl with black hair, who looked
about twelve years old.

"I am not a thief!" the girl said in
a low, angry voice. She was wearing a
red felt skirt, decorated with bands of
embroidery, and sturdy leather boots.

"We'll see about that!" the sales
assistant shouted, beckoning to a man
from another counter.

As Robyn stood at the far end of the
long clothes rack, the man hurried over.

"What's the problem?" he asked the assistant.

"This young lady has taken an expensive *lusekofte*. See, there is the empty hanger," the woman said crossly, pointing to the rack of knitted sweaters. "I demand that she opens her bag so that I can search it!"

"Did you see her take it?" the man asked.

The woman put her hands on her hips. "No. But she must have. One's missing, and it was there a minute ago!"

"I told you. I have not taken it. I would never do that," the girl said calmly, clutching her bag with two hands.

Her face was pale, expect for her cheeks, which were flushed a deep red.

Robyn could see that the girl looked
close to tears and admired the way she
was sticking up for herself against the
bossy assistant.

"That woman's determined to
search the girl's bag. I hope she hasn't
stolen anything," Robyn whispered to
Storm.

Suddenly, Storm's head came up,
and he gave a triumphant woof.

Diving beneath the rack of sweaters,
the tiny puppy jumped up and hunted
around. He grabbed something and a
loose sweater came free. Storm dropped
it on to the floor before padding back
to Robyn.

"Oh, well done, Storm!" Robyn
praised him, pleased that it looked like
the young girl hadn't taken anything.
"The sweater must have slipped off
its hanger. It was lucky you spotted a
bit of its dangling sleeve, Storm." The
sales assistant obviously hadn't looked

carefully enough.

On impulse, Robyn picked up the empty hanger and stepped forward. "Excuse me," she said politely, holding it up. "Are you looking for the sweater that was on this?"

The two assistants and the dark-haired girl turned to look at her.

"I know where it is," the woman snapped. "It's inside this young person's bag!"

"Are you sure?" Robyn asked. "Because there's one on the floor. Look."

The assistant frowned and went to investigate. A deep flush crept up her face as she came back holding the cardigan. "I . . . er . . . seem to have made a mistake. We'll say no more about it," she said shortly. Snatching the empty hanger from Robyn, she marched briskly away.

The male assistant threw the girl an apologetic look and then hurried back to his counter.

Robyn's eyes widened. "What nerve! That woman didn't even say sorry!"

"It does not matter," the girl replied,

shrugging. "I knew I had done nothing, but thank you for speaking up for me. I am Kristiana Magga. Everyone calls me Krista. What is your name?"

"Robyn. Robyn Parsons. I'm here on vacation with my mom and dad," Robyn said, surprised that the girl was so calm after the unpleasant scene. She saw that Krista had high cheekbones and unusual dark eyes, which were slightly tilted at the corners.

"I am very glad to meet you," Krista said with a wide smile.

"Me too," Robyn said. "Do you live here?"

Krista shook her head. "I am visiting friends. My Uncle Nikolai and Aunt Jorun are with me. Oh, here they are now."

A man and woman came toward them. Robyn saw that they had high cheekbones and dark hair, like Krista. Krista's aunt also wore a blue felt skirt and strong leather boots. There was a fringed gold shawl around her shoulders, pinned with a circular brooch.

"This is my new friend Robyn," Krista said.

Robyn glowed at Krista's description of her as a friend. Since they'd only just met, it was a nice thing to do.

Krista then told her aunt and uncle about the sales assistant who had accused her of stealing. ". . . and Robyn proved that I didn't steal it after she found the *lusekofte* on the floor," she finished.

It wasn't me, actually, it was Storm, Robyn thought, wishing that she could

tell them all how fantastic her magic
friend was. She smiled proudly at the little
puppy who was sitting nearby watching,
visible only to her.

"Thank you, Robyn," Krista's aunt
said. "It's very nice to meet you. I wish we
had more time to talk, but now we must
go."

"Yes. We have many things to buy before we return to our home in the north," said her uncle.

"Good-bye, Robyn," Krista said with a warm smile. "Enjoy your vacation."

"Thanks, I will. Bye, Krista," Robyn said.

She and Storm watched as the girl and her aunt and uncle left the shop. As they walked past the glass storefront, Krista paused to wave.

Robyn waved back, feeling a little sad that she had to leave so soon. "Krista seemed really nice, didn't she?" she said to Storm. "What a shame that we'll never see her again."

"I liked her, too," Storm woofed.

"Come on, Storm. Let's go and find

Dad." She no longer wanted to buy any presents from this shop.

Chapter
SIX

The next day passed quickly. *Sea Princess* sailed along through ever more majestic fjords, and Robyn and Storm stood on deck to watch the spectacular scenery passing by. When the ship docked at another coastal town, they went ashore with her parents to explore.

Before boarding again, she found time to dash into a shop and buy her mom

some traditional hand-knitted gloves.
She also bought her dad a wallet and
got felt slippers for her gran and gramps.
"Great. I'm finished with my present-
buying." *Except for Storm*, she thought,
wondering how she was going to buy
him a present without him seeing.

Later on Robyn, Storm, and her
mom and dad sat in a cafe near the
harbor.

Robyn stirred a blob of whipped
cream into her mug of hot chocolate
and then took a big sip. "*Mmm.
Delicious*," she murmured, licking her
lips.

Her dad grinned around a mouthful
of muffin. "I'm not sure a chocolate
mustache is a good look on you!"

"Ha-ha! Very funny." Robyn made a

face at him and wiped her mouth.

She scooped up a big fingerful of whipped cream and slipped it inside her shoulder bag for Storm to lick. His warm little tongue flicked over her fingers, and she hid a fond smile. She loved having Storm as her friend and sharing this wonderful vacation with him.

Robyn gazed out of the window as she nibbled a spice cookie and found herself thinking about Krista.

Robyn had told her mom and dad

about the sweater incident in the
shop and described Krista and Jorun's
beautiful clothes. "Your young friend is
probably from a Sami background," her
mom guessed. "I read in our travel guide
that the Sami people used to be known
as Lapps and once moved around with
their herds of reindeer. A lot of them live
a more settled life now."

Robyn remembered that Krista's
Aunt Jorun had said they were returning
to their home in the north. She thought
it must be amazing to live in a land of
ice and snow, where it got so cold that
even the sea froze.

Sea Princess docked at a small port
the next morning and Robyn, Storm,
and her parents made their way to a

smaller boat, which was waiting to take
them to see a large glacier.

Passengers piled into the boat and
lined the rails. Robyn looked down into
the dark, freezing water, which was so
much closer to them on this small boat,
and shivered. It looked very cold and
very scary—she held on to the boat rail
as it set off. On the way to the ice cap,
the vast, frozen expanse that stretched
its arms down into a number of deep
valleys, they sailed between islets and
skerries.

Robyn was waiting excitedly for her
first-ever glimpse of a glacier.

"We should see it in a minute," she
whispered to Storm, who was in her
shoulder bag.

Storm nodded.

Robyn was unprepared for the
amazing sight that met her eyes. The
frozen river, cutting through the huge
snowcapped mountains, ended in a
breathtaking wall of towering ice, which
was reflected in the sea.

"Oh my gosh!" Robyn's jaw dropped.
"That's awesome!"

Sounds of cracking, like pistol shots, rang out in the still air and some of the passengers looked worried. Storm whimpered, and Robyn glanced down to where he sat with his front paws looped over the bag. He was twitching his ears nervously.

"That noise is just the sound of boulders getting crunched under the ice," the guide explained to the worried passengers.

"Did you hear what that man said? It's nothing to be scared about," Robyn whispered reassuringly to Storm. But when he continued to stare at the glacier intently, she frowned. "Storm? Did you hear me?"

There was an extra loud *bang!* and an ominous grinding sound—Storm's

entire fluffy white body tensed, and his hackles rose along his back. "There is great danger!" he barked urgently, leaping down on to the deck.

Robyn felt a familiar warm prickling flow down her spine as big golden sparks bloomed in Storm's fluffy white fur and his ears sparked with electricity. Suddenly, the little boat shot forward in a dazzling burst of speed.

Robyn grabbed hold of the rail again and clung on for dear life.

Storm whimpered as his claws skittered across the deck, and he slid toward the rail, about to fall overboard into the freezing, bottomless sea.

Robyn acted without thinking. Still hanging on with one hand, she swooped down and reached out.

For one heart-stopping moment,
she thought she had lost Storm. But
then her fingers closed on the scruff
of his neck. Yes! Robyn hauled the
terrified puppy to safety and tucked his
trembling little form safely back inside
her bag.

"Thank you for saving me, Robyn!"

Storm barked, looking up at her gratefully with his big blue eyes.

"I'm just glad you're okay," she replied, trying to stay on her feet and steady her shoulder bag at the same time.

The other passengers were bracing themselves as best they could as the small boat suddenly zoomed back out to sea in a shower of golden sparkles before stopping abruptly near one of the small islets.

"Storm! What's going on?" Robyn asked in a shaky voice.

Suddenly, there was a thunderous cracking sound, and massive slabs of ice parted from the glacier and dropped into the sea with a resounding *splash!* To everyone's horror, a huge tidal wave began rushing toward the boat.

Robyn felt the color drain from her face as the wall of water bore down on them with the speed of an express train.

Storm calmly lifted both front paws and sent another fountain of sparks whooshing across the sea at the tidal wave, which immediately sank without a trace. The small boat rocked gently as normal-sized waves brushed harmlessly against its sides.

No one else could have seen Storm's magic, and the stunned passengers all began speaking at once.

Robyn looked down fondly at her little friend. "You were amazing, Storm! We could all have been really badly hurt, and you nearly were. Thank you."

Storm gave a little shake as every last spark faded from his thick fur. "I am glad I was able to help."

"Are you all right, honey?" asked
Robyn's dad, putting his arm around her
shoulders. "I'm a bit shaken up myself!"

"I'm fine now," Robyn said.

Beside them, Robyn's mom
shuddered. "I dread to think what would
have happened if we'd been right under

the glacier when that sheet of ice fell off! Thank goodness the captain had the presence of mind to put on a burst of speed."

"Whoever was responsible for saving us was very brave, wasn't he?" Robyn said meaningfully, reaching one hand into her bag to stroke Storm's warm fur.

She felt so proud of her friend. It was just a shame that no one else would ever know how wonderful he was.

Chapter
SEVEN

Robyn stood on deck, bathed in the night's moonlight, with Storm cuddled in her arms inside her coat. She was still a little nervous after saving Storm the other day and was determined to keep her little friend safe.

It had grown colder as *Sea Princess* steamed further north, and this was the coldest weather Robyn had ever

experienced. The icy air prickled inside
her nose as she breathed in. It was a
strange sensation.

Storm's ears were pricked up, and his
breath fogged in the air as he gazed up
at the millions of silver stars that seemed
so close you could reach out and touch
them.

"*Brrr!*" Robyn said, trying to hide a shiver. She was thinking of going inside to get warm, but the tiny puppy was obviously having such a good time that she didn't want to spoil his enjoyment.

"You are cold, Robyn," Storm noticed. "I will make you warm."

A familiar warm tickling sensation ran down Robyn's backbone as tiny gold sparks bloomed deep within his fluffy white coat. Instantly, she felt a thick layer of fur lining her jeans, her jacket, and even her gloves, and she was as warm as toast.

"Thanks, Storm, that's much better. Oh, look!" Robyn breathed in wonder as a shifting curtain of glowing greenish lights appeared and began rippling across the clear winter sky. "Those must be the Northern Lights. Aren't they amazing?"

"They are like the lights of my homeland. We often see them in the sky," Storm woofed softly, sounding a little sad.

Robyn wondered what Storm's home world was like. Perhaps it was a land of ice and snow, too. It must be a strange and wild place, where the great magical wolves that lived there fought over their lands. She felt a pang as she thought that Storm might be homesick and thinking of his wounded mother and the scattered Moon-claw pack.

Bowing her head, Robyn kissed the top of Storm's silky little head and held him close.

"Robyn? Is it really you?" called a voice.

Robyn almost jumped out of her skin. She spun round to see the slim, dark-haired girl from the knitwear shop standing there with a broad smile on her face.

"Krista!" she said delightedly. "What are you doing here?"

Krista smiled. She wore a red parka with a fur-trimmed hood. "I am on my way back home, with my uncle and aunt. I did not realize that you were on a cruise around the coast. We use the coastal steamers, like *Sea Princess,* as local ferries to get around."

Robyn remembered seeing that *Sea Princess* had a ferry and car deck. "Where do you live? Is it very far

away?" she asked, hoping that there might
be time for her and Storm to get to know
Krista better.

Krista told her. "We will reach the
port in two days, on Christmas Eve. My
village is a short distance inland. I live
there with my mother and father, my
brothers and sisters, my aunts, uncles and
cousins, and all the rest of my family.

I will be very glad to see them again."

"You live with *all* of your family?" Robyn asked curiously. She did get a bit lonely with her dad away a lot of the time, but Robyn wasn't sure she'd want to live with a whole lot of other people. "Do you travel around a lot after your reindeer herds? Sorry. I didn't mean to sound nosy. I'm just interested," she said, blushing as she realized that she seemed to be asking lots of questions.

Krista laughed. "That is all right. At this time of the year, we live in houses, but others, like my grandmother and grandfather prefer to live in a *lavvo*—that's a traditional tent," she explained. "Lots of other Sami families live in the village, too. We make things to sell, until the season for calves to be born, and then everyone helps out with the hard work."

"Cool," Robyn said, fascinated. Krista's life was completely different to her own. It sounded so busy and exciting.

Krista smiled at her enthusiasm and her slanted dark eyes twinkled. "Would you and your parents like to visit my village and meet my family?"

"Would I? I'd love it!" Robyn said at once. "But I'll have to ask my mom and dad if it's okay. They're in the main lounge. Why don't you come with me, and then you can meet them?"

Krista nodded. "I would like that. I will go and get Uncle Nikolai and Aunt Jorun. They would like to meet your parents, too."

As Robyn went belowdecks with

Krista, she whispered to Storm, "Isn't
it great that we've bumped into Krista
again?"

Storm's little face lit up, and he
woofed in agreement.

Robyn woke the following morning,
feeling full of excitement. Storm was
curled in the crook of her arm. As she
stirred, he opened one eye and then
tucked his nose back between his paws.

"Come on, sleepyhead!" Robyn
teased, gently tickling his furry little

sides. "We're meeting Krista for breakfast."

Storm stuck out all four fluffy white legs and had a big stretch before jumping to the floor.

Robyn threw back the quilt and got dressed quickly. Her parents were showered and ready, and they all went to the restaurant together. Robyn spotted Krista at a table the moment she and Storm walked in. She waved to her as she helped herself from the usual display of delicious food.

"Hi," Robyn said as she went and sat next to Krista.

"Hello, Robyn. Did you sleep well?"

"Yes, thanks. Oops," Robyn said, as she felt Storm scrabbling up on to her lap. She pretended to drop her fork and just managed to stop him from slipping off again.

The adults joined them with their plates of food. Mr. Parsons and Uncle Nikolai began chatting about soccer. Robyn's mom and Aunt Jorun talked about knitting, having discovered that they shared a passion for crafts the previous night.

"They all seem to be getting along very well, don't they?" Robyn commented to Krista.

"Yes, they do," Krista said. "I am very pleased that your parents have accepted my invitation to visit our village."

"Me too. I can't wait," Robyn said eagerly.

"I'm glad you said that," Krista replied, her eyes glinting mysteriously. "I have

told my cousin Morten that you are
coming to visit. He is arranging a surprise
for you."

Robyn smiled, wondering what it
could be.

Chapter
EIGHT

Later that day, Robyn and Storm were
walking past some fishing boats frozen
into the ice on a village wharf, on their
way to meet up with her mom and dad
who were in the supermarket. Robyn
couldn't stop thinking about what Krista's
surprise might be. She smiled down at
Storm happily—this was turning out
to be one of her best Christmases ever.

Suddenly, Robyn heard some furious
snapping and growling. It was coming
from a car parked outside a supermarket.
In the back were two large dogs, who
were scrabbling at the window.

Storm whimpered in terror and
cowered against Robyn's legs. She could

feel him trembling from head to foot
through her warm boots.

"Shadow knows where I am. He has
sent those dogs to attack me," Storm
whined.

Robyn tensed as she saw the
streetlights gleaming on the dogs' pale
eyes and extra large teeth. How was
she going to save her little friend?
She was just about to pick Storm up
and run away as fast as her legs would
carry her when a man came out of the
supermarket and got into the car. The
fierce growling and barking eventually
faded as the car pulled away.

"Those horrible dogs have gone now.
You're safe with me," Robyn said. She
picked Storm up and hurried onto a
narrow side street.

The tiny puppy pressed himself against her and looked up at her with fearful eyes. "For now, perhaps, but Shadow will use his magic on other dogs we meet. If any of them find me, I may have to leave quickly, without saying good-bye."

Robyn couldn't bear to think of losing Storm so suddenly. "Maybe if we hide you really well, Shadow will give up looking for you and then you can stay with me forever. I'll take you home with me when the cruise ends. You'll love it there."

Storm reached up and touched her face with one fluffy, white front paw.

"That is not possible. One day, I must return to my homeland to lead the Moon-claw pack. Do you understand that, Robyn?" he barked, his little face serious.

Robyn swallowed hard, but she forced herself to nod as she went back toward the supermarket. She didn't want to think about anything, except enjoying every single moment of her Christmas vacation with Storm.

Christmas Eve finally arrived, and Robyn and Storm stood beside Krista as *Sea Princess* steamed into the harbor with her horn blaring. The grayish winter light hung over the small town, which banked steeply up the hillside behind the harbor.

The ship was only staying for a few hours, as the Christmas festivities would soon begin on board.

"Will it take long to get to where you live?" Mrs. Parsons asked Krista.

"Not long at all." Krista looked at Robyn and her lips curved in another of her mysterious smiles.

Robyn was puzzled. What could Krista be planning?

Ten minutes later, when she and Storm were getting off the ship, Robyn gave a cry of delight. A beautiful wooden sleigh, pulled by two reindeer in brightly colored harnesses with woolen tassels stood waiting.

"Wow! This is fantastic," Robyn enthused.

"What a wonderful surprise," her dad said.

Krista smiled. "I thought you would like it. This is Morten, my cousin," she said, introducing the tall young sleigh driver.

"Pleased to meet you," Robyn said, smiling.

Robyn's mom and dad greeted him, and then Morten helped them climb aboard the sleigh, before helping to load the supplies.

Robyn settled Storm on her lap and they nestled beneath the warmth of the thick furs. Krista sat next to her. Once everyone was settled, Morten twitched the reins and the reindeer sped off across the snow in a jingle of sleigh bells.

"This reminds me of that "Winter Wonderland" song!" Robyn's dad said. "In the lane, snow is glistening. Can't you hear, logs are blistering . . . ," he

began, singing all the wrong words.

Robyn saw her mom give him one
of her looks and poke him in the ribs.

Robyn stifled a giggle as her dad fell
silent. Krista glanced at her mom, and
they both burst out laughing.

Storm sat upright on Robyn's lap,
looking around at the thick blanket
of white snow. More flakes began to
fall, dancing in the glow of the sleigh
lanterns.

Soon lights were visible in the gloom
ahead. Robyn saw buildings with grass

poking up through the snow on their roofs. Tall, cone-shaped tents were dotted around. She could smell wood smoke on the frosty air.

As Morten brought the sleigh to a halt, people hurried out to welcome back Krista and her aunt and uncle. Robyn smiled and shook hands as she was introduced to Krista's parents, her brothers and sisters, and countless aunts and uncles and cousins. She knew she'd never remember all of their names.

"My grandparents would like to welcome you to their *lavvo*," Krista explained. Robyn, Storm, and the adults were shown inside one of the tents.

Colorful wall hangings and a crackling log fire inside the *lavvo* made it very warm and cozy. Delicious smells came from

a metal cooking pot hanging over the
flames. Robyn sat down close to the fire,
and Storm came and curled up beside her.

Krista's grandparents made them
very welcome with food and hot drinks.
Afterward, a woman entertained them
with traditional chanting and storytelling,
while playing on a skin drum covered
with drawings.

"We call this *joik*," Krista told Robyn.
"Storytelling is an old tradition of my
people."

Storm sat up and pricked his ears,
enjoying the entertainment. "I like this
place," he woofed.

Robyn reached down to pat him, to
show that she did too. But she didn't dare
risk whispering to him with all the people
around.

Krista showed Robyn around her house, too. It was similar to the houses back home, with a modern TV and a computer, but there was a large wooden hut and a wooden pen for reindeer attached to the side of it. Krista's mom made fabulous jewelry with silver wire.

Time passed all too quickly and soon they had to return to *Sea Princess*.

There were many good-byes and hugs all around. Morten drove the reindeer sleigh back to the harbor, and Krista insisted on coming along with Robyn to keep her company.

As the sleigh drew to a halt at the harbor beside the huge bulk of *Sea Princess*, Krista slipped something into Robyn's hand.

"I made this. It is for you," she said.

Robyn looked down to see that it was a tiny reindeer-horn carving of an arctic wolf. The tiny wolf looked just like Storm as his real self. It even had chips of some glittery dark-blue material for eyes.

"Oh, it's beautiful. Thank you," she said warmly, giving Krista a hug.

"I am glad that you like it," Krista said, her tilted dark eyes moist.

"I love it so much," Robyn said with a catch in her voice. "Good-bye, Krista. And thanks for letting me meet your family. I had the best time ever. I'll send you an e-mail when I get back home."

Krista's face brightened. "Oh yes, please do. And maybe we can talk online. It will be wonderful to keep in touch with each other."

"Definitely!" Robyn promised. She wished this Christmas could last forever.

Chapter
NINE

Robyn stood on board *Sea Princess* with Storm in her arms. They were looking down at the harbor, where Morten was turning the sleigh around. The reindeer and Krista, huddled in the sleigh among the furs, looked tiny now.

Krista waved one small mitten as the reindeer plunged forward and the

sleigh moved smoothly away on wooden
runners.

"Good-bye. Safe journey!" she called.

"Good-bye!" Robyn cried, waving.

She and Storm waited until they could
no longer hear the sound of sleigh bells
before going inside the ship.

Robyn's mom walked beside her.
"Well, that was wonderful, wasn't it?

Krista's family was so hospitable. You must get me their address. I'd love to send them something from home when we get back."

Robyn thought that was a great idea.

"Well, shall we go and see if anything's happening in the lounge yet? I feel like singing a few carols," her dad said.

"Sounds great. I'll just be a minute. I want to get something from the cabin," Robyn replied.

She was going to grab the gloves and wallet, which were hidden at the end of her bunk. She wanted to wrap them and then sneak them under the enormous Christmas tree, so her mom and dad would be able to open them later.

Storm padded beside Robyn at her
heel as she went belowdecks. They had
just stepped into the corridor leading to
their cabin when Storm gave a yelp of
terror and shot forward.

"What's wrong?" Robyn said,
frowning.

Storm stood beside the cabin door,
pawing frantically at it. She could see that
he was trembling from head to foot.

Suddenly, Robyn heard fierce
growling. Whipping around, she saw the
shadows of two large dogs coming down
the stairwell on the wall behind her.

Robyn's heart missed a beat. Shadow
must have found Storm when they were
on land and sent his dogs onto the ship
after him! The puppy was in terrible
danger.

Robyn didn't think twice. She hurtled down the corridor and unlocked the cabin door with shaking fingers. She and Storm dashed inside, just as a fierce snapping and growling sounded right behind them.

"Oh!" Robyn shielded her eyes with her hand as a dazzling flash lit up the entire cabin.

Storm stood before her, a tiny fluffy white puppy no longer, but a majestic young silver-gray wolf. Hundreds of tiny diamond-bright lights glowed from his thick neck-ruff. Beside him stood a larger wolf with a gentle expression and large golden eyes.

And then Robyn knew that Storm was leaving for real.

She went forward and threw her arms

around the wolf's neck. "I'll never forget
you, Storm," she said.

Storm allowed her to hug him for
a moment and then gently pulled away.
"You have been a good friend, Robyn.
Be of strong heart," he rumbled in a deep,
velvety growl.

Robyn nodded, unable to speak as
she felt a tear run down her cheek. She
remembered that she hadn't been able

to get Storm a Christmas present. It seemed wrong not to give him something.

She had a sudden thought. "Please, wait!" Reaching into her pocket, she took out Krista's gift. She held it out to Storm. "This is for you. To remind you that, one day, you'll be a great leader of the Moon-claw pack," she murmured.

Storm reached out and closed his huge paw over the tiny carved wolf. "Thank you, Robyn. You are very kind."

There was a final burst of intense gold light and a great shower of gold sparks exploded silently into the air and drifted harmlessly down around her. Storm and his mother faded and were gone.

The fierce growling outside the cabin stopped and silence fell.

Robyn felt a deep ache. She would

never forget Storm, but she would always have her memories of the incredible Christmas vacation she had shared with the magic puppy.

The cabin door opened and her dad stood there. "Oh, there you are, honey. Are you coming up to the lounge? There's a carol service on, and afterward Santa Claus is going to hand out presents."

Robyn quickly wiped away a tear and smiled. "Just coming!"

About the
AUTHOR

Sue Bentley's books for children often include animals or fairies. She lives in Northampton, England, and enjoys reading, going to the movies, and sitting watching the frogs and newts in her garden pond. If she hadn't been a writer, she would probably have been a skydiver or brain surgeon. The main reason she writes is that she can drink cups and cups of tea while she's typing. She has met and owned many cats and dogs, and each one has brought a special sort of magic to her life.

Don't miss these Magic Puppy books!

Don't miss these Magic Ponies books!

Don't miss these Magic Kitten books!

Don't miss these Magic Bunny books!